Praise for . . . **Brock, Pik**

D1601319

that through the bonds of love from family and friends things can and will get better." CARNEGIE JUDGING PANEL ON *LARK*

"The quartet is a magnificent achievement and *Lark* is a totally fitting and superb finale. . . . Simple, yet immensely powerful writing of the highest order." JOY COURT, SLA, ON *LARK*

"As taut as Steinbeck's *Of Mice and Men*, *Lark* rings with truth, humor, humanity, and pathos." *NEW STATESMAN* ON *LARK*

"As ever, McGowan's understanding of masculine youth—its brashness and unexpected tenderness—is evident, and there is a quiet worldliness underpinning the whole." *LITERARY REVIEW* ON *LARK*

"Anthony McGowan's story of brothers Nicky and Kenny, which began in *Brock*, reaches a heart-rending but perfectly pitched conclusion in *Lark*." *OBSERVER* ON *LARK*

"It is funny, scatological, terrifying, heartwarming, and heartbreaking, and is written in everyday prose through teenage Nicky's convincing voice." *SUNDAY TIMES* ON *LARK*, CHILDREN'S BOOK OF THE WEEK

"A gripping story . . . the author's vivid writing and tense plot has enough pace and drama for this short novel to entertain any audience." *IRISH NEWS* ON *LARK*

"McGowan makes such complexity available to his teenage readers in a social context where day-to-day life can be abrasive and emotion is implicit rather than expressed." BOOKS FOR KEEPS ON *LARK*

"A deeply touching story. . . . Anthony McGowan maintains the intensity of the story throughout while also keeping the writing simple." LOVEREADING4KIDS ON *LARK*

PIKE

ANTHONY McGOWAN

UNION
SQUARE
& CO.

NEW YORK

**UNION
SQUARE
& CO.**

NEW YORK

UNION SQUARE & CO. and the distinctive Union Square & Co.
logo are trademarks of Sterling Publishing Co., Inc.

Union Square & Co., LLC, is a subsidiary of Sterling
Publishing Co., Inc.

Text © 2015 Anthony McGowan
Cover illustration © 2024 Christina Mrozik
Interior illustrations © 2015 Staffan Gnosspelius

First published in Great Britain in 2015 by Barrington Stoke Ltd.
First published in the United States and Canada in 2024
by Union Square & Co., LLC.

ISBN 978-1-4549-5479-8

Library of Congress Control Number: 2023942868

For information about custom editions, special sales, and premium
purchases, please contact specialsales@unionsquareandco.com.

Printed in China

2 4 6 8 10 9 7 5 3 1

unionsquareandco.com

Cover design by Melissa Farris

Union Square & Co.'s EVERYONE CAN BE A READER books are
expertly written, thoughtfully designed with dyslexia-friendly fonts
and paper tones, and carefully formatted to meet readers where they
are with engaging stories that encourage reading success across a
wide range of age and interest levels.

To Barry Hines, who showed us how this might be done.

ONE

Deep in the green murk, something stirred. It eased up from the weed and sludge at the bottom of the lake so slowly you'd think it was just drifting in the current. Only there was no current, and the lake water was as still as death. And if you looked closer, you could see the tiny ripples made by the fins, and the shimmer of energy that passed through the solid body under the scales.

Just enough light filtered through the water for the pike to see her prey. It was a minnow, dappled green and brown to conceal it as it darted among the weeds. But the minnow had abandoned the safety of the bottom, drawn by a new and unexpected object in the water. Something that linked the dark lower and the bright upper layers of the lake.

And now the minnow was a sharp outline against the morning light.

Close. Closer. It was time.

But perhaps the minnow had sensed danger, for he had swum into the cover of the strange new presence in the lake. One long branch of it reached up, almost to the surface, and that's where the minnow lurked now. He swam in and out of the five white bare twigs at the end of the branch, where bark frayed from the wood—or bone—beneath.

There the minnow made his fatal mistake. He nibbled once, twice, at the flakes of bark—or skin, perhaps—and as he pulled at the pale shreds, he ignored the coming darkness below.

And so the pike struck. There was simply nothing between the point at which she began her surge and the point at which she stopped. The minnow was gone, engulfed, swallowed. And with it, the tip of a little finger, severed by the teeth of the pike.

TWO

Even in my sleep I knew I was being watched. And because I knew someone was there, I was alert and tense and ready to spring as soon as my eyes were open. I must have been in the middle of some sort of horror dream, because I was kind of expecting zombies or vampires when I opened my eyes.

It was worse.

There was a black shape looming above me, dark against the light streaming in the window. The shape gave out a faint noise, like a hum or a moan.

"What the hell are you doing, Kenny?" I said.

Kenny was my brother. He was a year older than me, but his brain was starved of oxygen when he was getting born, so I had to look after him. There was a big drooling grin all over his face. The moaning sound was because he was trying his hardest to keep quiet, and that was the best he could do.

"You said I wasn't allowed to wake you up any more," he said, "so I was waiting."

"What time is it?" I said. It was the end of the summer break, and I was trying to make the most of the few days of rest I had left before school started.

Kenny picked up the alarm clock. The ringer had been broken for years, but that didn't matter with Kenny around. He touched the glowing numbers on the clock, his face dark with effort.

"Seven o'clock. A.M.," he announced, and grinned again. "Fishing time!"

I'd promised Kenny I'd take him fishing, and Kenny never forgot a promise.

"Okay, I'm up," I said. "But don't wake Dad."

"He's not home yet. He's on nights."

"Okay, make a racket then."

THREE

Ten minutes later we were off down the road with our Jack Russell terrier, Tina, yapping and scampering around our feet. The toaster was broken, so we just munched on slices of white bread as we walked along. I carried the fishing rod, and Kenny had the rest of the gear—the hooks and floats and maggots—in an old ice-cream carton. I didn't let him carry the rod because you never knew what he was going to do with it, and it was the one thing we couldn't afford to replace. It was my dad's old one from when he was a kid. Dad didn't make a big fuss about it, but I knew it was special for him.

We were going to the Bacon Pond. It's a funny name for a pond, I know. It's called that because it's right next to the Bacon Factory, where they used to make all sorts of meat pies and stuff, as well as bacon. It's closed down now—the Bacon Factory, I mean. Everything's closed down around here except the dollar stores and the pubs and the convenience store. I've heard people say they're going to turn the Bacon Factory into apartments for rich people, but I'll believe that when I see the Ferraris parked outside.

"Tell me about the pike again," Kenny said, as we walked.

One of the things about Kenny is that he likes to hear the same story over and over again. In fact, he never likes a story until he's heard it about ten times, and then he loves it, even if it's actually a bad story.

But the story about the pike wasn't bad.

"So you know about the Bacon Factory?" I asked him.

"Yeah, they used to make pies and ham and stuff."

"And you know what they did with the old meat that had gone rotten and nasty?" I asked.

"They used to throw it in the pond."

"That's right. And you know what used to live in the Bacon Pond?"

"Ginormous pikes!" Kenny said. "But stop asking questions and tell it properly."

I laughed. The truth is I liked telling stories to Kenny, because he really, really listened. He listened with every part of him, as if he could hear you with his legs and his hands as well as his ears.

FOUR

"Back when the Bacon Factory was still open," I told Kenny, "they used to dump the rotten meat into the deep, black waters of the Bacon Pond. The pond was jam-packed with fish. There were clever carp and lazy tench in the still, deep water, and silver roach darting in the shallows. And there were perch, like underwater tigers, prowling in and out of the weeds."

"Tigers!" Kenny said, and his eyes were as wide as if he was seeing a real tiger, and not just a little fish with stripy sides.

"But most of all there were the pike," I said. "You'd sometimes see a fisherman pull one out of the water, small ones, not much longer than a pencil, and not that much thicker. But sometimes there'd be one as long as a man's arm, and you could see the power in it, and the evil, because a pike'll eat anything it can.

"And there was talk of real giants in the deep, like this—" I stretched out my arms to show Kenny. "They were so fat and bloated that if you tried to hug one around the middle, your hands would barely meet. But the real giants had lived a long time, and they were smart, and no one could ever catch them."

Kenny put his arms around an imaginary pike.

"And it's not just that they get big," I went on. "There's something about the look of a pike, the way its jaws seem to go on forever.... You know the rest of it is just a machine for getting its mouth to the right place at the right time. It looks like a dinosaur, or an alien, or a monster."

"Monster," said Kenny.

Even Tina seemed to be listening, looking up at me as she trotted along.

"I knew a kid once who said he was feeding the ducks," I told them, "and this swan came floating over, like a white queen. But before it reached the bread it was gone, just like that. The kid swore that he'd seen the huge mouth come up under it, and

grab the beautiful head, and pull it down, and it never came back up again, not even a feather of it."

"Feather," Kenny said, in a whisper.

"There would never be enough food in the pond to feed monster pike like that, if it wasn't for the spoiled meat they dumped in there from the factory. And so the pike grew fat on that—on the old pork-pie meat and rotten sausages and green bacon.

"And sometimes a fisherman would hook something huge in the water, but they never had the strength to pull it in. Or the line would snap, or the rod break like a toothpick."

Kenny made a dry cracking sound with his mouth.

"So that was the pond and the pike," I said. "But there were also kids, and kids like to do dares. One of the dares was to swim across the Bacon Pond. Even without the pike, it was a stupid thing to do. In places it was so deep that if you tried to dive down to the bottom you'd come up, spluttering, before you reached it. Deep enough to drown, easy."

"I'd never swim it, no way," Kenny said.

And I paused the story for a minute and said to him, "Yeah, Kenny, you're right not to."

Kenny could swim, but just a scrappy sort of doggy-paddle, with his head held high in the water.

"But the deep bits weren't the real danger," I told him. "There were places where waterweeds could tangle you. And people used to dump all kinds of crap in there—dead dogs and cats, shopping carts, and baby carriages. There was even a car or two, burned out by joyriders, then pushed out with the flames still melting the insides of it, to fizz in the deeper water."

Kenny went, "Pssssssshhhhhhhiiiiiiiiiiisssssss-shhhhhhhh," and waved his arms around like the billowing blue-black smoke from a burning car.

"The shells of the dead cars and the wire from the shopping carts could snare you, and hold you there until you got tired and sank down," I told him. "Then, when you were dead, the eels would chew up your eyeballs and eat your brain, and the pike would tear the flesh off you, until all that was left was your bare bones and your teeth and your hair."

That was the bit that Kenny liked the best, and he didn't make any noises or do any actions.

No, not quite the best. The second best. We weren't at the best bit, yet.

"So, the dare was stupid," I said. "But kids *are* stupid. And there was one very dense kid called Vinnie Tuck. Vinnie Tuck was the terror of the town. He used to steal from the stores and break windows and run up to girls and grab them where they didn't want to be grabbed. He was always in trouble with the police, but not bad trouble, because his dad had loads of money and he always smoothed things over for Vinnie, the way you can when you're rich.

"Vinnie used to boast that he could swim across the pond as easily as he could piss across a puddle. And he said he was going to do it skinny—with no clothes on.

"So, a load of Vinnie's friends were there egging him on. He takes his clothes off, down to his undies, and then off *they* come, and all his friends give a cheer. It was springtime, March or April, and early

in the morning so it was pretty cold, and so his thingy looked like a little blue acorn.

"Then with a roar Vinnie Tuck splashed into the pond. He ran at first, where it was shallow, then slower when the water came up to his waist, and then he went into a crawl. And he was a pretty good swimmer, Vinnie, I'll give him that. Fast and steady, and he put his head right in, even though he didn't have any goggles.

"But it was chilly, like I said. And the chill meant that soon his body started to go numb. And then he got the fear—that sense that things were just . . . wrong. His stroke became less steady. The voices of his friends were fainter, as he got farther away, and as his ears filled with the slimy water.

"And then he felt it—something long, moving past his leg. That first time it might not even have touched him—it could just have been the water, moved by whatever it was. But it was enough to make Vinnie stop dead and tread water, so he could look around.

"Nothing.

"He started again, trying to get back up to speed. But now his strokes were frantic and out of control. The next time it really did touch him. He was numb with the cold, but still he felt it—felt it the way you do when the dentist gives you a filling, and it shouldn't hurt, but it does, it does.

"The touch of it was both smooth and rough. Smooth because all fish have that coating of slime. Rough from the scales. It passed right under his belly, and it took seconds, he felt, to shift its great length from one side of him to the other, like when you slide your belt slowly out of your belt loops.

"This time Vinnie didn't stop. This time he thrashed with more and more frantic strokes. But he did look down, and he forced his eyes to stay open in the stinging, oily water. And he saw them. Not just one monster, but dozens of them. Pike of all sizes, making lazy turns in the water, keeping up with him with no effort at all. Vinnie screamed, choked, coughed, screamed again. His friends had begun to run around the side of the pond so they could meet him at the far bank, and they sensed that something was horribly wrong.

"Now Vinnie wished he'd kept his pants on. Even in his panic he never thought—never *really* thought—that the pike would pull him down and eat him, the way a shark would. But now he imagined the pike, the big one, spotting his thingy flapping in the water like a maggot or a worm. He imagined the pike opening its mouth, with its hundred needle-sharp teeth. He imagined the teeth closing around . . .

"Vinnie was almost there. He tried to reach down with his toes, and he could just scrape the bottom, greasy with rotting weeds. Two more strokes and he'd be safe. At last his style came back to him. He reached forward into the water like an Olympic swimmer, going for gold. Then he pulled his hand back, to send his body surging forward like a torpedo. And then.

"*AAAAAAAHHHHHHHHHHHHHHH!!!!!!*

"The agony, the terrible agony.

"Fire.

"Ice.

"Fire.

"It was his *thing*. It'd got it. Teeth sliced, cut, crunched. The great jaws were twisting it free, the way a croc spins underwater to dismember the body of a drowned zebra.

"At last Vinnie's feet found the bottom again and he stood, staggered, fell, staggered again, splashed forward. He was screaming all the time, and his voice was going from a deep bellow to a high-pitched wail. He couldn't look, couldn't stand the thought of what was there.

"And then he saw the faces of his friends. They were laughing. They were pointing. They were doubled up, out of control. One actually fell in the mud and rolled around.

"At last Vinnie looked down. There it was, attached to his thing, holding on for dear life. A tiny pike, the size of a snapped pencil. It held on with teeth so thin you could almost see through them, and trickles of blood ran down Vinnie's legs to mingle with the green water and the mud and the duckweed that were stuck to him.

"If the sight of the tiny fish made his friends laugh fit to bursting, it had a different effect on

Vinnie. He lost his wits completely, running up and down the bank, too scared to even touch the fish. The last his friends saw of him was his bare ass as he ran back along the lane toward the town, still screaming out his banshee wail.

"In the town, people saw him running naked through the streets, and some thought they were imagining it, and some thought that they must be drunk. Most thought that it was Vinnie who was drunk or on drugs, but none of them saw the little fish. Maybe it had dropped off by then, or maybe it was just so much like his thing that they didn't notice it. And Vinnie kept on running till he was out of the town, and the last the town saw of him was that bare white ass."

"And what happened to him next?" asked Kenny. His wild laughter had suddenly gone, like a summer shower.

"Nobody knows," I said. "Some say he lives in the woods around here, and still has the little pike attached to him. I even heard that it's still alive, the pike. It's bigger now, and it lives like a vampire fish, sucking his blood, and it controls

him. But I also heard he went to live with his mom in Leeds."

And by that time we'd reached the Bacon Pond itself—the real one, and not the one in the story.

FIVE

In winter, when the cold rain whipped across the water and the trees stood naked and alone like black skeletons, Bacon Pond was a miserable sight. But now, at the end of summer, the weeping willows leaned over the banks, and reeds and rushes whispered, and swallows swooped so low down to catch flies that sometimes their wing tips would make a tiny splash, and it was a good place to be.

Tina thought so anyway. She sprinted up and down the bank on her little legs, and snapped and growled at invisible enemies.

"Keep that darn dog under control."

The voice came from a bit farther down the bank. It wasn't loud, but it had a menace in it that made it carry. I looked and saw a man hunched over his fishing rod—one of those enormous ones that seem to stretch out forever over the water. I couldn't see the man's face because the hood of his green parka covered his head. He didn't look at us as he spoke, but just kept staring out over Bacon Pond.

"Come on," I said to Kenny. "Let's move over to the other side."

I put the leash on Tina and we walked around on the muddy path. It only took ten minutes. On a Saturday there'd be loads of people here, but today the man in the hood was the only person there, apart from us.

The fishing rod and the reel were already set up, with the line threaded through the metal eyes along the rod. All I had to do was attach the float, the hook, the weights, and a maggot. I explained what I was doing to Kenny.

"You need the float to stop the line and hook sinking to the bottom and getting all mucked up," I said. "It goes here, above the hook. Then you need these little weights. You put them on the line under the float, so the line dangles nice and straight in the water. Then you tie the hook on. You've got to use a special knot, or it just falls off."

Getting the hook tied on was the hardest part. As I worked I heard a noise from Kenny. When I looked up, I saw that he was imitating me, sticking his tongue out of the corner of his mouth, which I always did when I was concentrating. I was annoyed for a second. Kenny was good at faces, and I knew he'd got me just right. And then he cracked up, and I cracked up too, and Tina barked like mad, like she always did when there was laughing or fighting going on.

SIX

Something made me look up then, when I had got the hook tied on the line, and I saw the man across the pond. He was standing now, staring at us. His hood had fallen back, and I could see his face. It was sort of blank, but you got the feeling he was trying to control some strong feelings that boiled up inside him. It felt kind of creepy, and I wondered if he was one of them bad men, you know, that bothers kids.

But then I thought that me and Kenny were old enough to take care of ourselves. Kenny could pick up the big cans of gas for the barbecue like they were tins of beans, and even my dad used to go red in the face when he tried to move them.

But that wasn't the point. There was something weird about the man, and he shouldn't have been staring at us.

Anyway, I wasn't going to let the creep spoil our day.

"Do you want to put the maggot on, Kenny?"
I said.

"No, you do it," Kenny said. "I don't like it."

Kenny played with Tina while I opened the old margarine tub that my dad kept the maggots in, pulled one out, and stuck it on the hook. I didn't much like doing it either. Some white sticky stuff came out of it, and I was glad Kenny hadn't seen it.

"I'll cast, and then you can do the catching," I said.

I saw Kenny trying to work out if I was cheating him out of the good bit, and then he nodded.

"Okay."

There was an island out in the middle of Bacon Pond. It wasn't very big—you could have spat from one end to the other if the wind was behind you. But it was all covered with trees and bushes, and so it had a kind of mystery. You could imagine having adventures there. Getting lost. Finding treasure. Being eaten by cannibals.

My dad had told me that the water around the island was the best place in the pond to catch fish. Of course, you couldn't get to the island without a boat. But if you could cast your hook out there, then you'd land something huge. So that was what you tried to do. And usually you failed.

I pulled the rod back and cast out as hard and as far as I could. It was pathetic—it didn't even go halfway. But it didn't really matter, not to Kenny anyway.

"Here," I said, and I gave him the rod to hold. "Just keep it steady for a few minutes, then reel it back in."

So that's what he did, while I sat on a tree stump and watched out for him. But that got boring after a few minutes, so I threw a stick for Tina instead. She loved that. She raced along like she was a lion or something, chasing zebras.

Then Kenny looked around. "Can I try casting?"

"As long as you're careful," I said. "And give me a chance to get out of the way."

You never knew where the hook was going to end up with Kenny, and I didn't want him to go fishing with one of my eyeballs on his hook. So I stood farther back and watched him.

Casting is tricky, because you've got to let go of the trigger thingy on the reel at just the right moment. Kenny's first attempt was terrible, and the hook and the weights and the float landed more or less at his feet with a plop.

I tried not to laugh.

I remembered what my dad had told me when he showed me how to cast, and that's what I said to Kenny.

"Imagine you're throwing a rock out into the water. You do the same thing with your arm, just don't . . ."

I was going to say "let go," but it was too late. The rod turned end over end as it flew through the air, with the line and float and weights and maggot still attached.

There's a story, about King Arthur and the Round Table, and Arthur's got himself sliced up, and he's dying, and he tells one of his friends to chuck his sword, Excalibur, in a lake. The first two times his friend thinks, Nice sword, no point in wasting it, and sticks it up his tunic. But Arthur sends him back, and the third time he chucks it in, and this hand comes out of the water and catches it. I almost thought that was going to happen now, with the rod. But it didn't. It just plopped into the water, out by the island. That would have been the perfect cast, if Kenny had kept hold of it.

Kenny looked at his hand, then back at the rod, then around at me, and then back at the rod.

"I've chucked it," he said. "It was an accident."

Even as he said it, Tina rushed past him and leaped into the pond. She wasn't one of those dogs you see splashing about any time they get the chance—in fact, I think she was a bit scared of the water, on account of her little legs that meant she'd be in up to her ass even in a puddle. But the rod was like a giant stick, and it was too much for her to resist.

"Tina's getting it for us!" Kenny said, excited. "Go on, Tina, fetch, fetch!"

Tina was already halfway to the island. It did almost look like she might bring the rod back, and I found myself grinning along with Kenny. It turned out Tina was a pretty good swimmer, and she was going like a torpedo.

But then Tina's ears pricked up and she stopped and looked about her. At the same time, I started to feel that something was wrong. I wasn't sure what it was, only that the water ... just didn't *look* right. And maybe I imagined it, but the world also went quiet in this weird way. It was as if the birds had stopped singing so they could watch, and the cars all fell silent on the road a few hundred feet away.

"What's Tina doing?" Kenny asked. "Is she playing?"

"I don't know," I said.

And then I did know.

There was something in the water with Tina. You could see ripples in the pond where there shouldn't have been ripples. No, not ripples, more a feeling of energy in the water. The sense that something was moving under there, in the darkness. No, not something. Some *things*.

Fish.

Big fish. I thought of the story of the swan, and how it disappeared. A swan was bigger than Tina.

I started yelling. "Tina, girl, get here!"

"What is it?" Kenny said. Fear made his voice go high and sharp. "Is it the pikes? Are they getting Tina?"

Tina had turned around in the water and had begun to paddle her way back to us. It seemed much farther now than when she'd swum out there.

I didn't know if the pike would really eat Tina, the way that sharks would eat anything. I was pretty sure the story about Vinnie was just a big joke, and that he'd run off for some other reason.

But there was the swan story, and that I did believe.

Tina was an annoying, yappy dog, and not that brainy, but she was our dog and we loved her, so I waded out into the water to help her.

It was shallow to begin with. It was two steps before it was over my sneakers. Two more and it was up to my knees. It didn't feel that cold, the way even the sea doesn't feel too cold when you're just paddling. But Tina was still far out of reach, and I could see the white terror in her eyes.

"Hurry up, Nicky!" Kenny wailed.

So I stepped out farther.

Knees.

Thighs.

Now it was cold. Colder still when it reached my undies. I can swim, but I'm not great at it. Whenever I try to do the crawl, I end up drinking half the swimming pool and crashing into some hard kid who gives me a thump. So I just do the breaststroke, like an old lady. But I didn't want to swim at all in the pond, didn't want to get out of my depth.

I was up to my chest now. Tina was trying to get to me. Her mouth opened as if she was trying to bark, but no noise came out. I could hear Kenny yelling behind me, but I couldn't make out what he was saying. Maybe it wasn't anything, no words, just a noise. And it almost seemed as if the noise of Kenny behind me was coming out of Tina's mouth, as if it was the little dog that was making that unearthly human cry.

All of a sudden I was afraid of the things in the water, the pike huge in my mind. I wanted to run back out of the water and get back home to Dad and our house.

But Tina.

I had to save her.

I pushed off from the slimy, muddy bottom and did two strokes, and she was there, in my arms. But that made things worse. I couldn't swim with her like that, all tangled up with me. She tried to scramble up on my head and her paws scratched at my face. I felt myself going down, and I thought, Shit, this is it. This is how I die, in the friggin' Bacon Pond, with a dog on my head like a friggin' stupid hat.

Then my feet landed again on the bottom, and the water was only up to my chin. I grabbed hold of Tina and lifted her up over my head and turned back, with dirty water streaming over my face and into my eyes.

And that was why I didn't understand at first what I was seeing. There was Kenny, just there. He'd taken a few steps forward into the lake, and the fear in his face was just changing to joy, as he realized Tina was safe.

But behind him . . . moving forward, and then freezing when he saw that I had turned. His hands still stretched out in front of him, as if he was about to grab Kenny.

It was the man.

The creepy man from before, who'd shouted at us. His face was full of . . . I don't know, rage, something like that. Something strong. Something scary.

I shouted, "Hey, Kenny, watch it, behind you!"

Stupid thing to say, as if we were in a play. And then I yelled at the man. "You get lost. Leave him alone."

Except that I didn't say "get lost," but something much worse than that—bad words, I mean.

Kenny turned around, and at the same time the man's face changed. It went blank and then he walked away with his shoulders hunched, pretending he'd just been strolling by.

But I knew he hadn't. I knew he was coming for us. Coming for Kenny. Coming for me.

I was out of the water and on the bank in seconds, and already the man had disappeared.

Kenny took Tina from my arms and she licked his face. I thought he was going to lick her right

back, but then she slipped out of his arms and galloped about on the side of the pond, glad to be back on dry land.

"Let's get home," I said, as the brown water dripped off me. My sneakers were so covered in mud it looked like I'd dipped my feet in melted chocolate.

"What about Dad's rod?" Kenny asked.

He pointed out toward the island. The rod was tangled up in a tree branch that stooped down to touch the water.

"Don't tell him about it," I said. "He'll be sad. I'll work out a way to get it back."

Kenny insisted on carrying Tina all the way home. She didn't seem to mind. She'd had a bad scare.

So had I.

The water, the man.

But something stopped me thinking about the bad things. Something I'd seen. Something... terrible.

And amazing.

SEVEN

Mick Bowen. He was the closest thing our town had to a real gangster. Stolen goods, that was his thing. Not stolen by him and his men, but by other people. Bowen owned a fleet of trucks and a couple of warehouses, so he could store things for other people, then ship them off around the country, or even farther away. I heard one of his main jobs was stealing top-end motorcycles, loading half a dozen into a truck and shipping them out to Russia.

Mick Bowen was a crook, but people didn't mind him. He lived in a big house just outside of town, and he used to buy drinks for people in the pubs. His son, Jez Bowen—called Jezbo by his friends— was a different matter. He was a thug, plain and simple. He hated me because I'd saved a badger he wanted to kill. But that's another story.

Anyway, Mick Bowen had got my dad into trouble last year. He made him store some stolen DVDs in our shed. It worked out okay in the end,

and my dad only got community service, but he could have gone to prison, and that would have got me and Kenny put into foster care. I'd have been all right, but it would have killed Kenny.

While Mick Bowen was out on bail after the DVD thing, he disappeared. Some people said he'd cleared off out of the country and now he was living it up in Spain or Brazil.

Then there were other stories. Some kid at school told me that the Russians had got him and chopped him up into bits so he didn't snitch on them.

I asked my dad about it, but he just shook his head. "Some things it's best not to know, Nicky," he said.

Well, now I knew.

While I was splashing around out on the pond, I'd seen something. Not the famous giant pike. It was worse than that. The waves I was making meant that something below the surface was exposed, just for a second.

It looked like a hand. A pale white hand. It was reaching up, almost as if it was that hand that

came up to catch King Arthur's sword Excalibur. That made me think that I'd imagined it, but I hadn't—it was definitely there. The water was too cloudy for me to see what was below the surface, but the rest of the person had to be down there. Maybe it was bundled up in something. It was probably weighted down at the feet, so it floated upright, with that arm stretched out, like the Statue of Liberty.

But that isn't what made me know it was Mick Bowen. That was the watch. It was the most famous watch in town. A huge gold Rolex. It was worth thousands. As much as a house. More than a house in our town.

All the way back home, my mind was racing. I didn't know how Mick Bowen had come to be in the Bacon Pond, if he'd drowned himself, or been murdered and dumped there. But I did know a couple of things. He was a bad man, and he'd got my dad into trouble. So he owed us. And that watch. . . . If I got my hands on that watch, I could sell it. I could give my dad the cash, and then all our money troubles would be over. We could get a new TV and a decent computer, and Wi-Fi, and the stuff that all the other kids had.

And it wasn't even really stealing. Bowen was dead, and dead men don't care what you take from them.

EIGHT

I was still soaked when we got home.

My dad spotted me in the kitchen, before I had
the chance to sneak upstairs and change. Dad
had just come back from his night shift at the
hospital. He always smelled funny when he'd been
working. A hospital smell. Disinfectant, sweat, and
something else. Sometimes he had to wheel dead
bodies around, and I thought maybe the smell was
the smell of dead people.

He looked at me, half serious, half laughing.
"What the hell happened to you?" he said.

My dad had been a bit messed up a while ago,
when he couldn't get a job, and after our mom
left us. Back then he wouldn't have noticed that
I was wet, or he would have starting yelling. But
things were better now. He had a girlfriend called
Jenny who was nice, and she'd helped him get the
job at the hospital. We were still broke, but me
and Kenny had clean clothes and proper dinners,

and there were always cookies in the jar, even if they were broken ones my dad got cheap from the market in Leeds.

"He swam in to save Tina from getting eaten by the giant pikes!" Kenny said, before I had chance to make something up.

My dad rolled his eyes and smiled, but then he looked more serious.

"How deep in did you go, son?"

"Not that deep," I said. "Just up to my middle."

"He didn't, Dad," Kenny said. "He was real brave. He went in all the way. He was swimming."

Kenny just wanted to be nice, to give me credit, but it wasn't the right thing to say.

My dad came over and put his hand on the back of my neck. He had big strong hands, rough from work, and you could feel the power in them even when he was being gentle.

"Look at me, Nicky," he said, and I did. I looked into his pale blue eyes. "It's dangerous. Kids have got into trouble there before, nearly drowned."

"I know, Dad."

"Stuff can tangle you. And you're not exactly Mark Spitz, are you?"

"Who?" I said.

"Oh, well, he was a famous swimmer before you were born," Dad said. "He won seven golds at the Olympics. Like that Aussie lad, the Torpedo."

"Yeah, Dad," I said.

"So promise me, then," he said.

"Promise you what?"

"That you won't ever go swimming in the Bacon Pond again."

"I didn't 'go swimming.'" I said. "I was saving Tina."

"Tina would have been all right," Dad said. "Dogs always are. And none of your smart answers. Promise me now."

His hand on the back of my neck was heavier. It didn't hurt—Dad never hurt us—but I could feel the weight of it. It felt like something important and big that I couldn't resist.

That makes it sound like a bad thing, but I knew it was a good thing. It was the weight of love, and you can't fight that.

"I won't, Dad," I said then. "I won't swim."

"You promise."

"I promise."

"Okay, go and get out of those clothes. You smell like frog shit."

That made me and Kenny laugh, and my dad joined in.

"There's enough hot water for a bath," he said, and off I went.

NINE

I had a nice long soak in the bath, and it gave me a
chance to work out a plan. My first idea was to go
back tonight, or early tomorrow, and swim out to get
the Rolex. I didn't love the thought of it, but with no
Tina climbing all over me, I reckoned I could do it.

But my dad had made me promise, and in a
way it was a relief. I was scared of what was in the
water, scared I'd get tangled, pulled down. And now
it wasn't just the giant pike that haunted the pond,
but the spirit of dead Mick Bowen too.

So I had to think up another way to get the
watch. A boat would be perfect, but I didn't have
a boat.

Then I had a brainwave. We had a blow-up
mattress thing—actually, a pool float—that we'd
got on vacation in Spain when I was a little kid.
I remembered that trip. It was hot and the sky
was blue forever. My mom was there, and Dad,
and Kenny.

But there was no point thinking about that. My mom was gone, and Jenny was okay. Better than okay.

The point was that the pool toy floated, and I could use it to get out to the hand and the arm and the watch.

So after my bath I got dressed in clean clothes (Jenny put stuff in the washing machine to make our clothes go soft and fluffy), and then I went out to the shed. It was jammed up with junk: boxes full of old toys from when we were kids, and magazines, and wires that you couldn't imagine ever connected up to anything.

The pool float was up on a shelf at the back. When we were little, me and Kenny used to get it down and dive on and off it in the garden. Kenny called it our bouncy castle.

But we hadn't done that for years.

It was dusty as heck up there on the shelf, and there were the empty husks of bluebottles and wasps and other stuff I didn't want to think about. A photo. A key from some other house. A letter.

Sometimes with bad things it's a good idea to think about them. When you think about them, you can make them better. But some things you just shouldn't think about at all.

So I dragged the pool float down, choking and spluttering from the dust and the cobwebs and the Kodak memories.

The float was blue on one side and red on the other. There was a grimy nozzle that you blew into. I wiped it and my fingers came away gray and furry. So then I spat on it, and wiped it again on my jeans. Then I started to blow into it, and after what seemed like a long time the blue-and-red plastic started to swell.

An excited voice came from behind me. "Are we doing bouncy castle?"

Kenny.

I should have shut the stupid shed door.

"No, Kenny," I said. "I'm just, um . . ."

And then, I don't know why, but I told him. Maybe it was those old sad things I'd seen and those old sad thoughts I'd had. It would have been more sensible to pick up Dad's old hammer off the floor

and hit myself over the head with it. But that's the thing about being a person—you do dumb-ass stuff the whole time.

"The thing is, Kenny, when I was out there, saving Tina, I saw something—"

"A pike?" he said. "A duck? A—"

He would have gone on shouting out random words for half an hour if I hadn't interrupted him.

"No, Kenny. I saw a dead man in the water."

"A dead man . . ." Kenny said. His face was yellow in the light of the bare hanging bulb.

And then questions came thick and fast into his head and out of his mouth.

"How do you know he was dead?"

"What did he die of?"

"Did he die of drowning?"

"Did he get eaten by pikes?"

"What's his name?"

"I don't know," I said, which answered all Kenny's questions together.

And then I went on, like the idiot that I am. "I mean, I might know who he was. Because I saw his watch. A gold Rolex. It would be worth more than our house. And I thought we could get the watch, sell it, and give the money to Dad. Then we wouldn't be poor any more, and Dad could buy stuff he needs, and we could go on vacation."

There was something else in the back of my mind, something I hadn't let myself *think*. If my dad was rich, then my mom might come back. One of the reasons that I hadn't let myself think this was that it felt like a betrayal of Jenny, who'd been really kind to us.

Kenny had been thinking while I was talking.

"It's that Mick Bowen, isn't it?" he said. "Jezbo's dad. Is he dead then? Is it him for definite?"

I nodded. "Yeah, he's the only person around here with a watch like that, and he's disappeared."

"Did the bad people get him?" Kenny asked.

"He was the bad people," I said.

"I mean really, really bad people?"

"Yeah, I think maybe they did," I said. "That, or he just fell in."

But I knew he hadn't just fallen in.

"You can't do that," Kenny said, after a pause. "It's stealing."

"It's not really stealing, Kenny," I said. "He's dead. And he owes us anyway."

"Why?"

"Because he got our dad into trouble."

I could see Kenny was worried by all this. He knew it was wrong, but he trusted me, and he always thought whatever I said was right.

"All we're going to do, Kenny, is get the watch off Mick Bowen," I said. "Then we can tell the police. We can phone them in a funny voice, so we won't get into trouble. They'll find him and get him out of the pond. We'll be heroes, sort of, but you can't tell anyone." I knew that would do the trick.

"Heroes," Kenny said. "Okay. Can we play bouncy castle now?"

I looked at the half-full pool float. "No, this is to use as a boat to float out to get the watch."

Kenny grinned. "Pirates," he said.

"Yeah, just like pirates."

TEN

Kenny looked at the float. "It's not very pumped up, is it?" he said.

He was right. I blew in some more. Then Kenny tried. Then I tried again. Any time we seemed to be getting there, it would go saggy again.

"I think it's got a hole in it," Kenny said.

"No shit, Sherlock," I said, which made Kenny laugh.

"No shit, Sherlock. No shit, Sherlock," he repeated, getting the sound of it into his head.

I scrunched up the float and threw it down in the corner of the shed. Kenny looked at it there, sad and useless. I don't know if he was remembering things too.

"We need a boat," he said. "A good boat. Not one with a hole."

"Yeah, but Kenny, this isn't the seaside. There's not even a canoe in this town."

"We could make one."

"Yeah, sure," I said. "Make a boat. That's easy, isn't it?"

Kenny didn't really get it when you were sarcastic. He always thought you meant what you said, like he did.

"Not a boat with sides," he said. "A flat boat. What do you call it?"

"A raft," I said.

As I said it, I started to get a bit excited. I remembered a film I saw on TV about some men who sailed across the ocean on a raft they made out of wood. *Kon-Tiki*, it was called. I'd wanted to make my own raft then, but I never did. I might have collected some sticks or something, but that was as far as I got.

I shook my head. "We haven't got any wood. Anyway, it'd take too long to make. Someone else is bound to find the bod—— to find the watch."

"Like that man who was there," Kenny said, and I remembered him, the man in the hood with the face at once blank and full of pain. "The bad man."

When Kenny said "the bad man," I thought about the other bad men who might have killed

Mick Bowen. Was the man who'd crept up behind Kenny linked to Mick? Had he killed him? He didn't look much like a Russian gangster. But maybe he was just some loser they'd got to watch over the body, to let them know if anyone found it.

All this should have made me think it was time to back off, to make that call to the police. But instead it just made me want to work faster.

"I know where there's some wood," Kenny said. "And it already looks a bit like a boat."

"What are you talking about, Kenny?"

"I can't remember what they call it," Kenny said. "Plates or something. In the factory."

I stared at Kenny while I tried to work out what the hell he was getting at. Wood like a boat ... factory. ... Then it hit me.

Pallets! The yard in front of the Bacon Factory was full of old wooden pallets—planks nailed into squares for shifting things on forklift trucks. Kenny was right. The pallets were basically rafts, and they were exactly where we needed them: next door to the pond. Perfect. Except ...

There were two problems with the pallets in the Bacon Factory. One was the big fence topped with razor wire that you'd have to get them over.

Well, one thing I've learned in my life is that there's always a way over a fence.

Two was the security guard and his dog.

The factory might be empty, but they still had security checking it. The guard wasn't there all day or anything, but he would turn up in his van at random times. I'd heard that if kids were messing around in the Bacon Factory when the guard turned up, he'd set his dog on them. I don't know if it was always the same guard, or the same dog, but that's how the story went. The dog was called Zoltan, and it was some kind of killer dog, fast and black. Everyone said that all its teeth were fangs, and if it got hold of you then you were dead.

Anyway, I knew some kids that Zoltan caught and he didn't kill them, but they always told the same story. Not to adults—to the other kids. They said the guard gave you a choice—you could either let him kick the crap out of you or he'd get the

police. That would mean you'd have a criminal record and probably get expelled from school.

One kid was supposed to have said, "Yeah, and then I'd end up with a shit job, like you." And the guard let wild Zoltan run out to the end of his leash, snarling and barking and gnashing his fangs. The dog didn't get close enough to bite the kid, but it was close enough for the kid to mess his pants. Or so everyone said. And after that the guard made the kid kneel on the ground while he slapped him about, gave him a broken arm, and kicked his ass.

Anyway, it might all have been bullshit, but that's what they said, and I didn't like it.

"What about the guard, and that dog Zoltan?" I said, half to myself.

"You need to distract them," Kenny said.

"What?" I didn't even know that Kenny knew a word like *distract*.

"Like in school, when you want to eat candy in class," Kenny said. "Kylie says, 'Miss, look out of the window, there's a rainbow,' and you put your candy in your mouth. Then you have to give a piece of candy to Kylie at break."

Normally I'd have taken the chance to tease Kenny about this girl Kylie, to say he liked her, and that sort of thing. But I didn't have time today.

"Okay," I said. "What do we do to distract the guard?"

Kenny puffed out his cheeks and waved his arms in a wide circle, and then he went, "Booooooooooooooooommmmmmmmmmmmm!"

ELEVEN

"Kenny, this is the weirdest thing we've ever done."

It was 9 p.m. and pitch black. Except, that is, for the floodlights around the Bacon Factory. There was the main building, which was made out of red brick, and then three or four smaller buildings, which were made of concrete.

It all looked a bit like a prisoner-of-war camp in an old film. Except we weren't trying to escape, we were trying to get in.

Kenny grinned.

He was grinning because of what was in the box.

We were crouching in some bushes not far from the road that led up to the gates of the factory.

"Right, Kenny," I said. "Tell me the plan one more time."

Kenny closed his eyes to help him remember, and he made his voice go serious. He knew I

wouldn't let him do this unless he was sensible. And he wanted to do it very much indeed.

"I have to wait here in case the man comes," Kenny said. "If he does, then I run around to the other side of the Bacon Factory, and I set them off. The man and his dog will go and see what it is. Then I run back here as fast as I can, in case you need help with the wooden thing. Then we go and hide it in the bushes."

He opened his eyes and smiled, proud of himself.

"And you'll be really careful?" I said.

"Really, really, really careful," he replied.

Kenny had his box, but I'd brought something too. It was a strip of moldy old carpet—something else I'd found in the shed. I jogged with it now toward the fence.

The fence was maybe seven feet tall, and perhaps I could have got over it, if it hadn't been for the razor wire at the top. It was like barbed wire, but instead of spikes it had these little blades. They were sharp enough to slice you up—like bacon.

Hence the carpet. I managed to hurl the strip up, so it draped over the razor wire. Then I took a massive run-up and got one arm up over it. I really wished the carpet was wider—if I put my hands a few inches on either side, I'd be going home without any fingers.

But there was no chance to think. One arm, then the other arm, then my leg, and then I was over.

That was when I heard the noise of the guard's van. I had to act fast. No way did I want that dog Zoltan tearing the ass out of my jeans, before that thug beat me up.

"Go on—run!" I yelled at Kenny.

He sprinted off along the fence. He needed to be quick to get around to the other side of the Bacon Factory and get set up.

The van backed up to the gates. The guard got out and opened the gate with a big bunch of keys. There was no sign yet of the dog, and I hoped he was sick or maybe retired. The guard got back in the van, drove in the gates, parked, and locked

up again. Then he opened the back doors and out jumped the devil dog.

I'd seen it before, but under the lights of the Bacon Factory it looked more evil than ever, with its giant tongue lolling out of its mouth like a demon.

The guard started to walk over to the main factory building. Sometimes I could see him, and sometimes he disappeared behind one of the smaller buildings.

I cursed myself for being such an idiot. Worse, for getting Kenny involved in this madness. I'd even let him talk me into letting him do the most dangerous part.

"I've done it loads of times with Samit," he'd said.

Kenny's friend Samit's uncle had a store that sold fireworks, and Samit always stole a few, so he had a whole lot of them, and him and Kenny used to go off to any secret bit of wasteland and—

A white line of fire soared into the sky on the far side of the factory. It rose in an arc, perfect, beautiful, and then burst into a flower

with orange-and-yellow petals. I sighed, the way you always do when the first firework goes up.

I also cursed. Kenny wasn't supposed to fire any rockets. It was meant to be low-down fireworks, plus bangers. He was supposed to set them up, light them, and get back here. I hoped he hadn't stayed to watch the stupid rocket head for the stars.

Then I saw it—a huge golden glow—and a split second later I heard the sound. It was a proper *boooooooooooooom* like Kenny had said. At almost the same moment I heard the dog go ballistic and knew I had to act. Now or never.

TWELVE

There were more bangs and fizzes as the fireworks went off, then a couple more rockets zoomed up from the patch of glowing brightness behind the factory.

I prayed Kenny was all right and wouldn't get caught by the blast or burned by a rocket going off the wrong way. I strained to see him, but the brightness of the floodlights made everything outside the gates too dark.

And then I heard his feet pounding toward me along the edge of the fence. I could also hear the glee—hear it in his very breath. A second later, his big smiling face was pressing against the diamond shapes in the wire.

"Did you see, did you see?" he hissed.

"You doofus," I said. "How many fireworks did you use?"

"All of them," he said. "And I put one in the box and lit it and then..."

"Yeah," I said. "Wait here. Do not move."

I ran over and grabbed a pallet. It was as wide as my arms, and hard to carry. It didn't seem too heavy, for the first few steps. But soon my arms started to hurt, and then, because I was holding it i n front of me and running sort of blind behind it, I stumbled and fell. My knee crunched right through one of the planks and I landed with all the weight on my fingers. I would have done quite a bit of screaming if I hadn't had to be quiet.

Would it work as a raft with the broken plank? Maybe, maybe not. But I wasn't taking any chances. I ran back and picked up another. I was more careful this time, running with it held sort of to the side so I could see where I was going.

Just before I reached the fence I heard something that made my heart stop.

Barking.

Distant.

Getting louder.

"Quick, Nicky," Kenny said. "Zoltan's coming. He's going to get you."

"Shut the heck up," I said, a bit harder than I should have.

Bark, bark.

Closer.

And then a shout, a human shout.

"Stand back, Kenny," I yelled, and then I heaved the pallet with all my might over the fence. It landed on the top, tottered for a moment, and then I jumped up and tipped it over, like a basketball player doing a slam dunk.

Bark, bark.

And another shout: "Zoltan, get back here."

The man had lost control of the dog. It wasn't going to be a beating. It was going to be a mauling.

I stepped back from the fence and ran at it. Fear made me strong. I got one arm and one leg over the top with that first leap.

But then disaster. The carpet should have been snagged on the razor wire. It would have been, if it had been barbed wire. But the blades weren't like spikes. They didn't catch. They cut and slid, and

the carpet slipped down inside the fence, with me
in a heap on top of it.

"Come on, Nicky, come on!"

I was up again. Over went the carpet.

"Hold the end of it on your side," I said, and
Kenny came over and did it. He looked along the
fence, back the way he had come.

There it was. The black monster, running
as fast as a racehorse. And behind it, the guard,
puffing and panting.

I ran back again and jumped. It wasn't as
good as my first attempt. I hooked one arm over
the top, but that was it. The dog was almost on me.
It was going to get me and drag me down and bury
its slavering snout in my belly and eat my guts.

I swung my right leg over. I felt the razor slice
the carpet, felt its hard edge cut my jeans, felt its
delicate edge begin to work its way into my flesh.
But I didn't care.

Zoltan was here.

Zoltan was leaping.

Zoltan's jaws closed on . . .

Thin air. With a snap like a cracked whip.

I was on the ground with Kenny pulling me up. Zoltan was going insane on the other side of the fence.

"Stupid dog, filthy dog," I said, and a few other things that I can't write down. And then we laughed our asses off crazy as we half carried, half dragged the pallet away from the fence and into the dark bushes around the Bacon Pond, three hundred feet away.

On the way home we agreed on our next steps. Tomorrow morning, we were going to come back and get that Rolex. It was our treasure. Ours.

THIRTEEN

I didn't sleep for more than ten minutes that night. I was buzzing. Buzzing with excitement. Buzzing with energy. Buzzing with fear. Buzzing from the adrenaline rush of nearly getting my undies chewed off by Zoltan.

We'd stashed the pallet in the bushes, but it wasn't very well hidden. So we had to go back early in the morning to finish the job. On weekends there were fishermen down by the pond from the crack of dawn, but not on weekdays. A few might come down later in the morning, and you'd get some kids messing around as well. So we didn't have long to do what we had to.

For once it was me waking Kenny. I watched him for a minute first. He always looked happy when he was asleep. You wouldn't think that someone could smile and sleep at the same time, but Kenny could. Not a big, stupid grin, but just

a half smile, like someone who knows an amazing secret.

I touched his arm. He didn't wake up, so I gave him a bit of a shake. Then he opened his eyes, looked at me in panic for a second, and then smiled again.

"Pirate time," I whispered.

He threw the covers off, and I saw that he'd gone to sleep in his clothes.

"Good thinking," I said.

Downstairs, Tina appeared in the kitchen. She was normally as yappy and bouncy as a puppy at the thought of going out, but I don't think she'd recovered from her scare of the day before. Maybe she could tell that we were going back to the pond, because she didn't start chasing around looking for her leash.

"Not walky time, Tina," I said.

Tina was one of the dumbest dogs you'll ever meet, so telling her stuff didn't normally have any effect on her. But this morning she turned around and went upstairs. I knew what she was up to. She

liked to sleep in the warm spot in the bed you'd just got out of. Mine or Kenny's, she wasn't picky.

I grabbed some bread from the bread box, and we ate it, raw and cold and clammy, on the way to the pond. The sky was the darkest blue you can imagine, with the stars still shining in it.

FOURTEEN

We reached the pond before sunrise. It was cold and still and quiet. The world was just light enough for me to make out the trees and the bushes and the water.

The pallet was where we'd left it. Me and Kenny carried it around to the far side of the pond, where we'd been fishing the day before. I could see the island sticking out of the water.

"That island looks like you in the morning," I said to Kenny, and I ruffled his hair. "With your hair all over the place."

Kenny stared out over the water. "Can you see the dead man?" he asked.

"I think you could only see it . . . him . . . his arm, I mean, when a wave moves the water," I said. "Anyone could have found him. Okay, let's get this thing launched."

The pallet was on the mud, and I thought it would slide in easily, if I shoved it with my foot. I was wrong.

"Give us a hand," I said to Kenny, and together we pushed and kicked and heaved it in. Like I said, the water was very shallow near the shore, and it wasn't deep enough for the pallet to float.

In my head it was all real easy. I thought I'd just slide the raft in, and it would float like *Kon-Tiki*, and then I could step onto it from the shore. But it was turning out to be a lot trickier than that.

After getting drenched yesterday, and ruining my best sneakers, I didn't want to get wet again. But I realized that there was no choice. At least I had my old, crappy sneakers on. Well, I didn't mind, as long as it was only my feet this time. I splashed out into the water, shoving the raft ahead of me with my foot. It moved a little easier now that the water was starting to lift it.

"Should have worn your boots," Kenny said from the edge.

"I haven't got any boots. And if I did, I would take them off and throw them at you."

"Don't be a grumpy head," he said. I'd never heard him say that before. He must have picked it up at school. Only it sort of rang a bell with me too. Was it something Dad used to say to him when I was small? Or maybe not Dad, maybe . . .

At last the raft was floating. Sort of. It didn't look quite right. I thought more of it would be up above the water, but it was so low that the waves I made by splashing about were washing over the top layer of planks.

But I kept thinking, It's okay. It's wood. Wood floats. Boats are made out of wood.

"Are we being pirates yet?" Kenny said.

"Yeah, nearly," I replied. I had a vague feeling there was something I'd forgotten, and I didn't want to step onto the raft until I remembered. Annoyingly, it was Kenny who thought of it.

"Paddles," he said. "For paddling."

I felt like an idiot. But I didn't want to own up to it.

"We don't need them," I said. "We'll just use our hands. It's not far."

In fact, now that the time had come, the island did look quite a long way away.

"I'll jump on it first, then you can join me," I said.

"I'm not in any hurry," Kenny said.

I looked over at him, and he had on a face I hadn't ever seen before. He was looking around as if he was really interested in the trees and bushes, and his face was oddly blank. I thought for a second he was going to start whistling, only Kenny didn't know how to whistle.

Then I realized what it all meant. He'd checked out the raft, and he didn't think it was going to work. For the first time in his life, Kenny didn't want to do something—and the reason was that he'd worked out that it was stupid.

I was kind of happy and sad at the same time. But also a bit annoyed. I was determined now to go and get the watch, and the fishing rod, and make Kenny think I always knew what I was doing.

"Kenny, you better stay here and keep a lookout," I said. "If any baddies come, you shout to me, okay?"

"No shit, Sherlock," he said.

Then I noticed that the raft had begun to drift away from me. It was now or never. I jumped, and I landed right in the middle of it. Just for a second I felt like a surfer on the ocean, with my arms out and my legs bent at the knees.

And then, with an impact that was too gentle to be a jolt, I realized that the raft had sunk down and settled in the mud at the bottom of the pond. I stepped off the raft and up to my knees in water, and the raft rose out of the sucking mud. I stepped on it again, and it sank down to the bottom.

I heard a sound behind me.

"If you're laughing, Kenny, I'll smash this pirate ship right over your head."

"No shit, Sherlock."

Then I couldn't carry on being serious. It was too stupid. I was laughing as well.

I dragged the raft back into the bushes—I didn't want to leave it there on the side of the pond. It

would be like a big black arrow pointing to the treasure. I was thinking again about trying to swim out to the watch. Maybe not now. I'd want my swimming trunks and a towel ready. But even as I was thinking that, I was also thinking that I was never going to do it, because I'd promised Dad. I realized that our dream of riches was over.

"We need to make it more floaty," I said to Kenny. "If we could shove something airtight in between the two layers of planks, it should make it floaty enough to carry me."

"Carry *us*," Kenny said, in a matter-of-fact way. "You promised I could ride on it."

"Well, yeah," I said. "But you didn't seem to want to just now."

"I could tell it was a bad idea."

"Thanks for letting me know."

Kenny smiled. "Miss says you only learn things when you do them. So sometimes you have to try it even if you screw it up."

"You are annoying sometimes, Kenny." I smiled. "Okay, let's hide this stupid thing, and get home before Dad's back from his shift."

FIFTEEN

We made it back before Dad was home, and we both went back to bed. Tina was under my duvet and I pushed her out, as I didn't much like being in bed with a dog. She went slinking off to Kenny.

Ten minutes later I heard Jenny's car pull up. She had a crappy little Toyota that sounded more like a lawn mower than a real car, and only the driver's door opened, so she always had to get out first and then let my dad out.

Jenny wasn't fat, but she wasn't thin either. She had one of those faces that looks like it's smiling even when it isn't, but it was okay, because she nearly always was. I mean, it would have been tricky if she looked like she was smiling when she was about to belt you one. But I don't think Jenny had ever belted anyone in her whole life.

She used to know my dad when they were at school, and she sort of saved him when he was in

a mess after my mom had gone. She helped him get his job and she sorted him out in other ways too. She didn't live all the time with us, but she stayed over quite often, when they were on the same shift together.

My dad liked his job, but it was tiring—he used to work nights half the time and days the other half, so he didn't know if he was coming or going.

I heard him pound up the stairs. He slammed his fist on my door, but I could tell that he wasn't mad or anything.

"Up you get, you lazy bums," he said in the loudest voice you could use that wasn't a shout. "I'm starving, so we're having a big breakfast."

I heard Kenny cheering from the next room. He sounded like a one-man soccer crowd.

My dad wasn't the best cook in the world, but he could make a mighty good breakfast. Twenty minutes later we were in the kitchen, with plates full of bacon and eggs and sausages and fried bread and fried tomatoes. Well, Kenny didn't have any tomatoes—he always says "they look like eyeballs," and I sort of see what he means.

My dad was always happiest when he was making a big breakfast. He had a tea towel over his shoulder because he'd seen some chef on TV do that, and he had this stupid apron with a picture of a body builder in his underwear on it, so it sort of looked like my dad's head was on this massive body. He had four pans all frying at the same time, and he was jiggling and rattling them to keep the eggs and bacon and everything from sticking.

When my dad was really happy, like now, he'd sing opera kind of songs, except with made-up words, either English words or just nonsense ones that sounded a bit Italian.

Jenny was watching all this and she was laughing like crazy, and Kenny was joining in with the singing. Now Kenny is great in many ways, but not even I, his best friend and his brother, would say that he was a good singer. In fact, Kenny's singing is like a goose and a dog having a fight.

Anyway, it was all brilliant, and everyone was happy, and then, for some reason, I said it. I don't

know why. Maybe it was the photo in the shed.
Maybe it was because it's me that's got something
wrong with my head, and not Kenny. Or maybe it
was because happiness makes me sad.

What I said was, "Dad, where's Mom?"

SIXTEEN

The fierce noise—the clattering pans, the rattling
plates, the singing, the talk—all stopped. Dad
looked at the floor. Jenny looked out of the window,
at the morning rain. Kenny stared at me with his
mouth open.

"She went away, son," Dad said.

"I know, Dad. But where did she go?"

"Just . . . away."

"Why did she, Dad?" That was Kenny.

I hated myself for starting this. But there's
no way of putting words back in your mouth
once you've let them out. It's like trying to put
toothpaste back in the tube.

"She couldn't cope," Dad said. The light in the
kitchen was too bright. It was making his eyes
sparkle.

"There was a kid at school," Kenny said. "He
said it was me. He said it was because I'm special."

"It wasn't you, Kenny," Dad said. "It was everything. It was me, as well. I should have . . . I don't know. There's things I should have done different. She loved you, Ken, she did."

"So tell us where she is, Dad." That was me again. "You must know. Someone must know."

"She wasn't from around here, Nicky," Dad said. "And she didn't have much family. She went back down south, I think. And we moved out of the old house. Do you remember the old house?"

"Not really. Sort of. There was a tree in the yard."

"We had a swing," Kenny said.

Kenny was a year older than me, and sometimes he remembered things that I didn't.

"We jumped off the swing onto the bouncy castle," he said.

Jenny was looking at my dad now. Even *her* face looked sad.

"You could try to find her, love," she said, her voice as soft as rain. "For the boys. Just to see. . . . I wouldn't . . ."

My dad shook his head. "I wouldn't know where to look. I heard she'd maybe gone abroad. Anyway, it's too late. It's too . . . gone."

Suddenly my dad looked old. He tried to undo the string on his stupid apron, but his fingers couldn't get it, so he pulled it over his head, and it got caught up and tangled.

"I'm tired," he said, and he went upstairs.

"Did you even try to find her, Dad?" I said after him. "Did you try at all?"

"I hate you," Kenny said, to me, I think. And then he went out as well, and I heard the shed door scrape open and then scrape shut again.

"You should go and see if he's all right," Jenny said. "I'll tidy this mess up."

"I'm sorry," I said to Jenny. "I didn't mean to . . . I just . . . I think I thought I should ask, while everyone was in a good mood. I didn't mean it to end up like this."

"Your dad does his best, you know," she told me. "He's a good man."

I nodded. And then I went out to see Kenny.

SEVENTEEN

"What are you doing, Kenny?"

He was hunched in the corner of the shed, holding something in his arms.

"Go away."

I went over to him. I wanted to say sorry. Or say something.

Then I saw what he was doing. He'd blown up the pool float and he was squeezing it in his arms, as if it was something precious.

I put my hand on his arm. He shrugged it off.

"Leave us alone," he said.

Where we're from, people sometimes say *us* when they mean *me*, but the way Kenny said it made me think he did mean *us* and not *me*.

He wiped his face with his sleeve, smearing snot and tears together.

I felt a lump in my throat like I was trying to swallow a walnut.

I tried to put my arm around him, but Kenny flailed at me. He was a strong kid, and when he got angry he could do some damage. I didn't mind getting hurt. In fact, a part of me wanted him to hurt me, to punch me in the mouth, to knock me out. But I knew he'd be even more upset when he realized what he'd done, and I didn't want that to be my fault as well.

So I left him there in the shed, hugging the pool float bouncy castle, thinking, I suppose, about the things that we'd lost.

I didn't know what to do with myself, then. I didn't want to be in the house, and it was too cold to wander around. I looked in my pockets. Four bucks and some change. Not even enough to get into Leeds and back.

So I thought I'd go to the library. I could look on the internet for ways to sort out the raft.

*

The library lady was kind of old-fashioned. Strict, but nice. She used to tell me what sort of books I'd like. She sometimes got it wrong, but other times it was as if she had read my mind. You could tell that

she wasn't too big on people using the computers, but she put up with it because it got kids into the library.

Usually she'd say something like, "I've got something for you, Nicholas," but today she just looked up at me from behind her desk. There was a man with her. He had that kind of soft hair like a baby's, and it was moving around in the breeze from the heater, and he had a brown jacket on that looked like it was made from dried horse manure. I wondered if the library lady was going to pack it in, and if the man was going to replace her. I'd have been sad if that happened.

So I went straight to the computers and googled about rafts and pallets. Most of the stuff there was about how you could join pallets together to make a big raft, and then use oil drums and that sort of thing to keep it afloat. But that was no use to me. I did see one raft that was a bit like ours, but it had blocks of polystyrene under the boards of the pallet, and I didn't know where you could get polystyrene, or if it was the kind of thing you could even buy.

And then I did something I'd never done before. I googled my mom, just in case. Her name's Yvonne, so I put in "Yvonne Lofthouse," and there were 56,500 results. I clicked through a few pages, but there was no one who could have been my mom. Then I realized she might not even be called that anymore. I mean she might have gone back to her own last name, whatever that was, or got married again and changed it to someone else's.

So I went back to the pictures of rafts and tried not to think about anything.

Then I heard a voice behind me. "This is one of our regulars. He comes in every week, don't you, Nicholas?"

I turned around, and the library lady was there with the baby man in his horseshit jacket. He looked like he'd have given all the money in his wallet to be somewhere else.

"This is Mr. Catterall from the council," the library lady said. "He thinks we don't need to have a library here. What do you think, Nicholas?"

I felt sick to my stomach. I wanted to say that I loved it in the library, that it was the best place in

the town, and that they should shut everything else down before they shut the library, but I couldn't think of the right words.

"We've got to find the money somewhere," Mr. Catterall said. "You've got a computer at home, haven't you, young man?"

"He comes in for books, as well," the library lady said. "Not just the computer. He's got a brother with learning problems. He helps him, don't you, Nicholas?"

I still couldn't get my mouth to work. I felt all the badness of the day piling up around me, and bursting out of me at the same time. It was like I was under the water of Bacon Pond, and it was crushing me, and I was swallowing it, and I was filled with it. Like a balloon, like a drowning man, like a dead body. I got up, and the library spun around, and I tried to run to the door but I hit a chair, then another chair, and I sent them crashing around me, like white waves on the water. I heard a voice behind me, the library lady, but I couldn't understand her, and then I was outside, and the sweat on me turned icy cold.

Everything was turning to shit. I knew, somehow, that the watch was wrapped up in this, that the watch was to blame. And that made me want it more. I was like one of those drunks you see staggering around outside the pub, the ones who drink to forget that they're an alcoholic.

EIGHTEEN

Nine o'clock. P.M., as Kenny might say. No stars tonight, no moon. A sickly yellow glow came from the distant Bacon Factory, but the light did nothing much—in fact, it made the trees and bushes around the pond darker, denser, like sweat on a black T-shirt.

I'd brought the taillight from my bike. The front light would have been better, but that had got stolen ages ago. The taillight cast a weak red beam, so everything it touched looked like a scene from a horror film, but without it I'd never have found the pallet.

I hauled it out from the bushes and got to work. I'd had a brainwave about what to use to help the raft stay afloat. Plastic milk bottles. I'd scrounged a trash bag full of them from a trash can behind the kids' playground. Most of them had been scrunched up, and I didn't feel like having to blow

into them to get them back to the right shape. But
I found enough with their caps on to keep the raft
afloat.

I managed to get about ten bottles in the space
between the top layer of planks and the bottom
layer, wedged in various ways. I wouldn't have
liked going down a raging torrent with rapids
and rocks and all that, but all the raft had to do
was get me seventy feet out to where I thought the
body was.

I knew I was going to get soaked, so I didn't
bother messing around this time—I just waded in
and dragged the raft behind me, still holding the
bike light in my left hand.

I looked back and it seemed to be working. The
raft was floating much higher in the water.

I put my foot on it. It wobbled. I staggered. I
realized that this was going to be difficult, even if
the stupid thing stayed afloat. I put the taillight
in my mouth, held the raft steady with both hands,
and tried to jump on. The raft tipped right up,
and dumped me ass first in the freezing pond. I

staggered up, gasping, and saw that half the bottles had popped out and were floating about on the pond like mutant ducks.

All day I'd been feeling like I was wrapped in a thick blanket of nothingness. But now I felt the rage and hopelessness and despair burst out of me, and I yelled out something—not words, just noise, because the light was still in my mouth—and I slapped my hands down hard on the crappy raft, like a baby does when it doesn't like its food.

Then, as the raft floated a few feet away, and as I stared dumbly at it, a voice came from behind me.

"That's garbage, that is. You need a bouncy castle."

I looked around, and I saw Kenny standing there. He had the pool float in his arms. All the foul things that I'd been thinking and feeling fell away, and I was just here with my brother, and we had a job to do.

"But it's got a hole in it, Kenny," I said. "The air won't stay in."

"Fixed it," he said, and he started to blow it up.

"How?"

Kenny kept on blowing, and I felt a bit stupid, still standing there in the water.

He finished, and the pool float was as tight as a drum.

"Puncture repair kit," he said, in a matter-of-fact way. "For the bike. I squeezed the bouncy castle till I felt the air blowing out of the hole, then I put the special glue on it, then I put the patch on it, then I waited. And now it's fixed, see?"

And it was.

I waded out up to my knees and got the raft back.

"We should let the air back out," I said, "then we can put the bouncy castle in between the two layers of wood."

And that's what we did. Kenny squeezed the air out, then we threaded the deflated pool float in between the layers of the pallet, then Kenny blew it up again.

This time, when I pushed it out, it sat high and proud on the water.

"That's a real boat," Kenny said. "A bouncy castle boat."

"It's great, Kenny. It was a good idea. Now you hold the taillight while I go and find the treasure."

NINETEEN

"No, I'm coming. I made the bouncy-castle boat."

And then Kenny was striding out into the water. I knew I should try to stop him, but I couldn't. I felt I owed him. Maybe this would balance out the stupid way I'd brought up our mom in the morning, and ruined what could have been a really nice day.

And maybe something in me, something scared, wanted my big brother with me. I know I'd always taken care of Kenny, because he was special and not that brainy, and so I kind of acted like I was *his* big brother. But the truth was that *he* was *my* big brother, and sometimes I needed him more than he needed me.

But if I'd been thinking straight, I'd still have said no.

"Okay, Kenny, I'll hold it steady while you get on."

It was easy with one person holding, and Kenny was soon on the raft. It was lower in the water, but not too bad.

"Now you," he said, and he held out his hand.

I thought I was going to pull us both into Bacon Pond, but somehow I got on the raft without turning it over. There was only just enough room for the two of us, and it sank a bit lower in the water, but it still floated.

Once the raft had stopped rocking, and we'd found the balance of it, I realized I'd done it again.

"Friggin' paddles!" I said.

Kenny grinned. "You'd forget your head if it wasn't screwed on."

That was another saying he'd got from Dad. He reached inside his coat and pulled out two Ping-Pong paddles. I recognized them from years before, when we used to play on the kitchen table with a net made of all our cups lined up across the middle of it. The paddles were almost completely bald now—just a few scraps of pimply rubber covered the thin wood.

The sight of them made me giggle, and I was worried I was going to lose control and tip us in the water for sure, but then I saw Kenny's serious, proud face and I got a grip.

"Genius," I said, and took one of the Ping-Pong paddles. "Pure genius. Best boat paddles ever."

I got Kenny to paddle on one side, while I did the other. The Ping-Pong paddles weren't that much better than hands would have been, but our hands would have frozen solid and we'd have got frostbite.

I shone the light ahead of us, and the island was there, dark and looming, just beyond the reach of the beam. Off we went, inching our way across the water.

I started to shiver. I think it was the fear and excitement as much as the cold.

"Do you want my coat?" Kenny said. "I'm not cold. I'm never cold."

That wasn't really true. Kenny would never remember to put his coat on, even if it was snowing. He'd be fine for a while, but then he'd go blue.

And then I thought that Dad, or Jenny, must have made him put his coat on tonight. That worried me. Kenny was terrible at secrets. If Dad had asked him where he was off to, he'd have tried to hide it, but it would have come out.

"Does Dad know you're here, Kenny?"

"No," Kenny said. "He went away somewhere with Jenny. He went in the daytime when he should have been sleeping."

I felt another stab of sorrow. Why couldn't I just have kept my stupid mouth shut? We were doing okay without Mom. We didn't need her.

I'd picked the scab, and now it was bleeding all over us.

Well, I couldn't help that. But I could get the watch. It wouldn't make everything better. But it might help. Money always helped, when you didn't have any.

TWENTY

So we inched over the still water of Bacon Pond, and the world was silent apart from the gentle splashing of our Ping-Pong paddles.

I looked up and saw that the sky was clear and full of stars, and I thought I'd like to learn their names because I didn't know a single one of them. Then I looked at Kenny, and even without the light I could see his face, and I thought it might have been because of the starlight, and that was a special thought. The thought, I mean, that I was able to see from light that's come from billions and billions of miles away, to shine here on my big brother.

But then I realized it was only the light from the old Bacon Factory, and that was a less special thought.

We were close now. I took the light out of my pocket and shined it across the water. Its beam

bounced and shattered on the ripples, so the water looked like it was burning.

"Like fireworks," Kenny said.

It was also like the glint of gold from a $30,000 Rolex.

We'd set off from the same place I'd jumped in the other day, and I hoped that if we went in a straight line we'd hit the spot where I'd seen the watch. But it was harder than I thought. The raft didn't want to go in a straight line, and in the dark it was almost impossible to know if we were on the right course. I tried to remember where I'd been when I saw the watch—what the island had looked like, which of the trees and bushes were nearest to it. But everything was different in the dark, and the feeble beam from the bike light didn't help much.

And now, here in the darkness, with light glimmering from the taillight and the stars, I began to wonder if I'd really seen the watch and the arm and the heavy body reaching up from the murky depths. I'd been panicking, splashing around,

gulping a frothy mix of air and water. All I'd really seen was that glint of gold.

"Keep your eyes peeled," I said to Kenny. As I said it, I wondered where such a dumb saying came from, and then I realized that the best place to find out would be the library, and that stupid man in his stupid jacket was going to close it down.

And so I was thinking about that, and also thinking that maybe it was time to forget this whole crazy scheme. I could go back home with Kenny, make us both something to eat, watch some TV, and then get to bed. And that's when I heard my brother yell out, "Found it! Found it!"

I turned around on the raft and saw Kenny stretching out, far over the side. I also saw what he was reaching for. Not the gleaming gold Rolex watch, but a stick. . . . No, not a stick—it was my dad's old fishing rod that Kenny had chucked in by mistake, which started this whole thing off. I'd got so obsessed with the gold watch that I'd forgotten about the rod, a precious thing from my dad's past. It was floating, but it had snagged on something.

"Kenny, careful . . ." I said, as he reached even further out toward the rod. But it was too late.

Perhaps it was always too late.

Too late from the moment I'd let him get on the raft.

Too late from the moment I'd come down here.

Too late from the moment I'd brought up my mom.

Too late from the moment Kenny had let go of the rod.

He fell.

There was hardly even a splash, because he was already reaching so far out. And as he fell, his feet pushed back against the raft, and that sent it, and me, shooting off the other way. And I'd been on one side of the raft, with Kenny on the other for balance. Once he was off, there was no way I could stay on.

The raft tipped up, and I was in the water.

TWENTY-ONE

As soon as my body hit the water, I felt a jolt like I'd been zapped in the electric chair. I gasped and flailed around, trying to get my arms on the raft, but all I did was slap at the water.

The bike light was gone. I saw the red beam spiraling down like a fallen star. The world was black.

"Kenny! Kenny!" I yelled, or tried to yell, but my mouth was full of water.

I fought the panic. I had to be calm. Had to save Kenny. I began to tread water, keeping my head above the surface.

"Kenny," I yelled again, clearer this time. "Kenny, where are you?"

I saw the raft floating many feet away. How had it got there? I could see the pool float, the bouncy castle. But no Kenny.

I screamed louder, not really to Kenny this time, but to the world.

"Help, please, help!"

And then I heard something. A gulp, a splutter. It was on the other side of the float.

"Kenny, I'm coming."

I swam—not any stroke you could put a name to, more like what an animal would do if you threw it in the water.

My clothes were heavy. I couldn't feel my hands, or even my arms. My jacket was in the way. I heaved it off.

"I'm coming, Kenny, I'm coming."

I was almost at the float. And then I felt it. Something was holding me. My jeans, my leg. I thought, for a second, of pike, of the huge pike. Its teeth in my leg. Then, as I turned and kicked and tried to reach down, I thought about the man in the water, the man we'd come here to find.

Mick Bowen.

The ghost of Mick Bowen.

Mick was a violent man. If you wronged him, he'd wrong you right back, wrong you all the way to the hospital. He was angry. He always got revenge. I screamed, not to Kenny, not to get help for Kenny,

but for me, and I felt the ghost of Mick Bowen pull me down. His arms were around me, holding me close. His arms, his legs, his body.

He wasn't a ghost—he was a zombie, a living corpse. His body had rotted down to rags. Rags and bones held me, and I looked into the rotted face, and saw the empty eyes writhing with worms, and worse than worms. The baby pike were in there too, evil like the slender knives of a torturer as they darted to and fro, nipping at the scraps of flesh around the nose.

And now the water closed over me, and all I could think of was Kenny. Kenny, who needed me, and who I'd betrayed.

I looked up and saw the starlight glitter on the surface of the water above me, and I reached up for it, as if the stars could save me, I held the starlight and it was as heavy as gold, and when I tried to pull it down with me, it wouldn't come. The starlight was snagged on something . . . on a branch under the water, its fingers trailing the surface.

A breath—and then agony. It seemed that there was one part of me that could still feel pain—my

scalp. My hair was being ripped off, torn from my head.

The dead man.

No, the monster pike. They were tearing at me, the huge jaws gaping to take in my head, scraping across the hard bone of my skull.

And all of a sudden I was above the water, held, dragged. I was on my back, my arms still waving, clutching at the water, at nothing. My mouth was full of water and filth. I wanted to cough, but instead I puked. I turned my head so that the stuff that came up didn't flow back down again, and I saw that the dead man, the ghost, was solid, hard as a rock fallen from the sky, and that's what he was. The star was a shooting star, a falling rock, and it had taken the shape of a man, of a monster.

Then I was on the side of the pond and my guts were heaving and writhing like the pike that had eaten the head of the dead man. I wanted to be dead, because of Kenny, because I'd killed him, my brother, who I loved.

And then I saw him, the ghost. Not the awful ghost of Mick Bowen, but the ghost of my Kenny.

He leaned over me, shook me, and behind him was the ghost of Mick Bowen, huge, hooded, his skull eaten away.

And then everything was flashing light and blaring noise, the red-and-blue light of hell and the jabbering of devils. I deserved the hell, deserved the devils. Only it was Kenny, Kenny who was still leaning over me, dripping on me, dripping the cold water of Bacon Pond and the hot water of his tears.

"Wake up, Nicky," he cried. "Wake up now!"

And then a man and a woman in green clothes lifted me onto a gurney and wheeled me to the ambulance.

TWENTY-TWO

I wasn't really with it in the ambulance. Kenny was in there with me. They'd wrapped him up in one of those silver blankets, so he looked like a giant turkey, ready to go in the oven. His hair was lank and filthy, and his face was streaked with mud. I suppose I looked worse. I saw that Kenny had the stupid fishing rod. I could have laughed, but it might have killed me.

I tried to work out what had happened.

Speaking was hard. My chest hurt, and my throat was raw from puking.

"Was it you, Kenny?" I managed. "Did you drag me out?"

"I helped the man," Kenny said. "He got me out first, but I was okay. I had hold of the bouncy castle. I fixed the puncture really good. Then he went and got you. He had to swim a bit, and he pulled your hair."

"Man?" I said. "What man?"

"That man. From the other day. That weirdo. I don't think he's a baddy. I didn't know you could get weirdos who are goodies, but you can."

"Don't talk, son," the ambulance man said. "There was a lot of water in you. I think you've got a bit of hypothermia as well. Really cold out there, to go for a swim." He was one of those men who've gone a bit bald and so they shave all their hair off to hide it. When he laughed you could see he had one of his teeth missing on the side, and I wondered why he didn't get a false one or something, because that looked way worse than being a bit bald.

He asked Kenny some stuff, but I don't know if he got much sense out of him, except that my dad worked at the hospital, but not the one we were going to.

Then we were at the hospital and they wheeled me to a room. Not a real room, just a cubicle with curtains across it, and Kenny came as well.

We were only in there five minutes when a nurse came to see us. She had a quick check of Kenny, and said, "You're right as rain, aren't you,

love?" And Kenny blushed, because she was quite young, and she looked nice.

Then she took the blankets off me, and touched my arms and legs, to make sure nothing was busted. She asked me if I'd bashed my head, and I said no. I was shivering like a jelly in an earthquake, but apart from that I was okay.

Then she took my hand.

"What's this here, love?" she asked. I looked down and saw that my fist was clamped around something complicated, slick, and heavy. I opened my hand and saw that it was Mick Bowen's gold Rolex.

"Oh, it's your watch," the nurse said. "Don't lose that. It's a nice one."

I don't think she'd understood what it was. It was still filthy from the pond and at first glance, like that, it maybe looked like a cheap knock-off.

"I'd put it on if I were you," she said. "If you leave it down in here, someone'll steal it!"

Then she was out of there. Kenny came over and stared at the watch.

"Is that it?" he said. "I never thought it was real."

I was still lying down. I felt too weak to sit up. I brought the watch close to my face, and looked at the back. There it was, Bowen's name, engraved in fancy writing.

It felt lovely, almost alive in my fingers. The way the strap moved, the heavy golden links flowed like a lizard over my hands. The face of the watch was an intense blue, darker than a blue sky, more like the flash of blue you see on a mallard's wing.

I thought about how nice it would be to keep this thing forever. To have it as my secret. To take it out in the night and hold it, breathing in its golden magic.

Then I thought about how I could sell it, and the things that we could buy with the money. We could buy peace and happiness and the end of worry.

And then I thought about the body in the lake. And I thought about the wife of Mick Bowen. And I thought about his son, Jez Bowen, who was a bully and a thug, and cruel. But I guessed that his dad loved him, the way that my dad loved me. And Jez probably loved his dad as well, as much as I loved mine.

"Can I hold it?" Kenny asked.

I gave it to him, and he held it and stroked it the same way I had done.

"I'm going to give it to Jez," I said.

Kenny looked at me. I thought he'd be angry or annoyed, or just not get it.

But he got it.

"Yeah."

"And I don't want to tell the police about it," I said. "I mean about how Jez's dad was in the lake. Not till I've told Jez."

"Yeah, I know," Kenny said.

"So let's just tell Dad that we went for the—"

"Fishing rod," he said. "I know. We did. I got it."

Just then my dad came in, with Jenny close behind him. He kissed Kenny, and hugged me, and called me an idiot, and he said if I ever did anything that stupid again he'd . . . well, he didn't know what he'd do. Then Kenny said it was his fault for losing the rod, and that I was only trying to stop him from getting into trouble. And when Kenny said that I felt proud and ashamed at the same time, because I couldn't ever remember Kenny telling a white lie before. He always told the truth, and sometimes he told fibs when he thought he was in trouble. But this was a lie he told to save me.

And then I told my dad about the man who'd saved us, me and Kenny both.

"We thought he was a weirdo or something," I said. "He shouted at us one time, and I thought he wanted to hurt us. . . . But then, well, I don't know why he was there, but we'd fallen off our raft, and I thought Kenny . . ."

And then I started to cry, and I thought I'd never stop.

But I did, in the end, and I finished the story. My dad asked me more about the man, then he looked thoughtful, but he didn't say much else.

TWENTY-THREE

They made me stay at the hospital that night. I was fine, but they said they had to keep an eye on me. I quite liked it. They have really comfy beds in the hospital, but the food's crap.

There were old people in the beds on either side of me, and one of them cracked jokes all night. "There were these two TV antennas on a roof, and they got married. The wedding was shit, but the reception was fantastic!" That sort of thing. But the one on the other side of me was dying, so he didn't have a great sense of humor.

I was okay the next day, and Dad and Kenny and Jenny came to collect me. There was also a surprise waiting for me outside the door of the ward. It was the man, the man from Bacon Pond.

"This is Mr. McGilligan," my dad said. "You've probably got something to say to him, I reckon."

The man smiled. He didn't look like he was used to it. Smiling, or talking to people for that matter.

110

"Thanks," I said, but then Kenny barged past me and hugged the man.

"Yeah, well," the man said, and not much more.

"The paper'll be after you, you know," my dad said, and the man sort of smiled again.

"I sure hope not."

Jenny asked him to come around one day for tea, and he said he would. Then we shook hands like grown-ups, even Kenny, and said goodbye.

Because of what had happened, I got the front seat in the car, and it was funny to see Dad and Kenny in the back, with their knees up around their ears.

"I worked out who that man is," my dad said. "I was at school with him. We called him Mog back then. He was all right to begin with, but something went wrong with his life, and he turned into a bit of a recluse. Lost touch with his friends. Never really settled. I always got the feeling something terrible happened to him, but I never knew what it was. Sometimes life just gets too much for you. Anyway, I went to see him last night, and I think helping you two might be the thing that . . . I don't know, brings him back from the edge. You never know."

Even though my dad was talking about this man, Mog, or whatever his name was, I sensed that there was something else going on as well. I could tell from the way Jenny was driving. She looked nervous, and she kept looking at my dad in her rearview mirror.

There was something . . . wrong. No, *wrong*'s not the right word. I mean more that things weren't normal. Something had happened. Not me and Kenny and the pond. Something else. Something that had to do with Dad and Jenny, as well as me and Kenny.

I don't know why, the trip in the car tired me out. I just about got up the stairs without my dad carrying me. I lay on my bed and my dad tucked me in, and I went to sleep until the afternoon. When I came downstairs, Dad and Jenny were in the kitchen, and Kenny was watching TV.

We chatted for a bit, and I told them I was okay. Then Dad said, "Yesterday I went back to the old house."

He stopped then, as if he didn't know what to say next.

"Go on," Jenny said. Not because she didn't know what was coming, I thought, but because she did know.

"I don't know if you remember the old house," Dad said. "It was nice. Bigger than this. The yard was ... It had a nice yard."

"The swing," Kenny said. He'd come in and was listening like it was a sport.

Dad smiled. "Yeah, that's right. The swing in the tree. That's not there anymore. Well, the tree is, but not the swing. This old couple bought it."

"The swing?" Kenny said.

"No, son, the house," my dad said. "Our old house. Well, they were quite old then. Really old now. But they're still with it. Not, not confused or anything."

I sensed that my dad was waffling a bit because what was coming up was hard for him to say. I had no idea what he was getting at. No, that isn't true. I knew it must be something to do with my mom, and what I'd said yesterday.

Yesterday? It seemed more like a hundred years ago.

"They remembered me, they did," Dad went on. "Surprising, that. Well, I suppose it might have been because of the trouble. The thing is, Nicky . . . Kenny . . . The thing is, your mom, she had some problems. She wasn't quite right, after, well, after she had you two. She had this bad thing called postpartum depression. It made her a bit sad. And I wasn't as much help to her as I should have been. I didn't really know what was going on.

"Anyway, she left. Just went off one day. We'd had arguments and whatnot, but I didn't think she was going to go like that. I sort of went to pieces a bit then too. I didn't pay the mortgage on the house, and the bank took it back. That's how come we had to move. I didn't leave the new people with an address for us. And I never . . . I never thought to get in touch with them. I mean, why would I?"

My dad stared into space for a few seconds. It wasn't hard to guess what he was thinking.

"I probably could have found your mom," he went on, sadly, "if I'd really tried. But it wouldn't

have been easy. The thing is, your mom didn't have much family. She never knew her dad, and her mom—your granny—she died a long time ago. She had a sister, but she was in Canada. Anyway, I wasn't thinking straight either, like I said. You boys know that. Not till Jenny here came along and sorted me out."

Jenny put her hand on his arm and smiled at him. He put his hand on top of hers. But he still looked sad.

"So I went there yesterday," he said. "After what you said, Nicky, I went to the old house. And it was hard. We were happy there, a lot of the time. So when I rang their bell, I was crying, tears falling off my face. They must have thought I had lost it. Surprised they didn't call the police on me.

"But they didn't. They invited me in for some tea, after I told them who I was. Because, you see, they had some . . . things. Part of me knew they might. And they did."

"What things, Dad?" I thought it, but Kenny spoke it.

"Letters."

And then my dad reached under the kitchen table to a plastic bag, and came back up again with his two big hands full of envelopes.

He put them on the table, and it was like this program I once saw about a fishing boat. The fishermen pulled up a net full of fish, then emptied them onto the deck, and when they spilled out there seemed so many more of them, millions . . .

"I haven't opened them," Dad said. "They're all addressed to you two. I think there's two each a year, birthdays and Christmas, going by the dates. And they're all from Canada. The old people in the house, they didn't have our new address. But they kept them. Kept all of them. I thanked them as best I could. Wish I could have done more."

I looked at the pile of letters. Neat handwriting on the envelopes, and strange foreign stamps. And then I felt my head go funny. I tried really really hard, but I couldn't stay on the hard kitchen chair, and I fell on the floor and went to sleep.

TWENTY-FOUR

The Bowens lived in a big house just out of town. It wasn't an old house, but it was made out of stone to make it look old. There was a wall around it, and a gate with spikes on top, and then a gravel path up to the door. It wasn't like the door to a normal house, but more like the door to some other kind of building, a bank or a church.

I rang the bell. It made an old-fashioned "ding-dong" sound.

I didn't know who would answer it. Jez Bowen lived there with his mom. He had a sister, but she was older and lived somewhere else. I didn't know if they were rich enough to have servants. A butler or something.

Jez opened the door.

He was a big guy, lean and hard. The Bowens had money, but they weren't posh. Jez was a thug, and he'd smash your face in if you got in his way

or on his nerves. I'd got in his way and on his nerves a lot.

His eyes widened when he saw me. He half smiled, and then the smile went away, and his hard face was back. I'd be lying if I said I wasn't a bit scared.

"What do you want?" he said.

I'd thought of a story. It was a bad one, but it was the best I could do.

"I was fishing up at Bacon Pond," I said.

Jez laughed.

"Why should I care what you were doing? Put it on effing Facebook."

"When I was there, I found something," I said. "Well, caught it. My line got snagged, and when I got it reeled in, this was on it."

I held out the watch.

Jez stared at it, his mouth open. The silence stretched out for what felt like ages.

"It's got your dad's name on it," I said at last, and I turned the watch around to show the writing on the back.

Jez took the watch from my hand.

"Never thought I'd see this again," he said. I thought he was speaking more to himself than to me.

"I think, I don't know, but I think he might have been . . . in the water," I said.

Jez looked at me, as if he had no idea what I was going on about.

"Huh?"

"I think I saw something," I said. "Someone. In the pond. And your dad's not . . . Maybe you should call the police."

Had Jez really not heard the rumors, the stories that his dad was dead? Could he not connect the dots?

Then Jez started to laugh. At first it sounded like someone trying to make themselves laugh, and I thought it might be a kind of crying. But soon it was a proper laugh, and Jez was bent double, holding his guts like he'd just got a boot in them.

I felt more stupid than ever, standing out there in the drizzle, with Jez laughing his head off. I should just have gone to the police and told all this to them.

Jez wiped his eyes with his sleeve.

"I last saw this a year ago," he said. "My dad told me to get rid of it. It's got his name on it, and he was skipping bail, leaving the country. He didn't want nothing that could identify him. So I chucked it in Bacon Pond. Only for a little nothing like you to fish it up again."

"Chucked it?" I said. "But it's a Rolex. Worth...loads."

"Yeah, sure," Jez said, his voice dripping sarcasm. "My dad used to get hundreds of these from China. It's just a shitty knock-off. He used to scam people the whole time with it. 'See how good they are,' he'd say, 'even I wear one, with my name on it and everything.' He used to tell people that he had a man on the inside of the Rolex factory who smuggled them out to him. All bullshit. Like I said, Chinese knock-offs. Here, have it. Then buzz off. Breathe a word of this to anyone, and I'll tell them Russians who are after my dad that you know where he is. They'll cut your balls off and make you eat them. Then they'll peel you like an orange, and every time you say you don't know anything, they'll slice off another strip. Now get lost before I start the job off for them."

And Jez Bowen slammed that heavy door in my face.

TWENTY-FIVE

I don't want to talk much about my mom's letters, except to say that she'd tried, for years, to get in touch. She thought that it was us who had rejected her. She was living in Canada, near her sister, and had a new life, and we had a half-sister out there.

We spoke to my mom on the phone. It was really hard. I don't think Kenny understood what was happening. No, that's not right. He understood it in a different way.

It was hard for my dad too. But Jenny was there to help, like she always was.

We're going to see my mom, in Canada, in the summer. Kenny's excited about going on a plane. So am I.

"You can watch films all the way," Kenny said. "They bring you special food on a special plate with a different place for all the kinds of food."

It's sort of a happy ending, I suppose. Except it isn't an ending, but just a way of going on.

The only endings are when you're dead, at the bottom of Bacon Pond.

So what did I see in the water? Was there a body? Or was it just weeds and branches and trash, and my mind turned it into Mick Bowen?

The man, Mog, comes around sometimes to see my dad. He's still a bit weird, but okay when you get used to him. And he saved me and Kenny, really saved us. The story was in the paper, and Mog was a kind of hero. He saved us and he found himself. It's like I said before. Until you're dead, there's always a chance you can make things a bit less shitty.

I wore the watch. It was a reminder of how low you can let yourself slip, of how low you can go. I'd look at it, or just feel its weight on my wrist, and I'd think, That was nearly a bad thing I did, almost stealing a dead man's watch. Of course, if he wasn't dead, then it wasn't stealing, just picking up some trash that had been thrown away.

Also, I'd never had my own watch before, and it told the time really well.

When I first got it out of the pond, it wasn't
working, and I thought the water must have ruined
it. But then it just started again. I had to tell my
dad the story of it—or at least a story that was as
close to the true story as I dared to go, right up to
Jez Bowen telling me to keep it.

My dad looked a bit odd, then he laughed too.

"I'm glad old Mick's not dead," he said. "He was
all right, for a gangster."

And he took the watch and said, "Really heavy.
I suppose the fake ones don't use new high-tech
stuff to make them lighter. Battery's probably a
bit flaky from being in the water. Go into town and
get them to put a new one in for you. They'll take
a couple of links out of the strap as well, so it fits a
bit snugger."

He gave me twenty bucks to cover it, and I got
the bus into Leeds.

I went into one jeweler's, but the man there
looked at it and said he didn't have the right
tool to get the back off. He told me to go to this
other place. It was down an alley and it was the
kind of place you'd only find if you looked for it,

and maybe not even then. It was mainly a shop for watches, but there was other stuff in the window: music boxes and clockwork toys from the olden days.

The man behind the counter looked annoyed when I came in. But that might just have been his face. He was one of those people who could have been forty, or could have been a hundred.

"Do you sell batteries?" I said. "For watches?"

"Yes, batteries," he said, and his voice sounded German or Polish or something. "Always batteries. What happens when you are alone and lost and your battery runs out, eh?"

I didn't know what to say to that. So I just said, "I need a new battery for this," and I gave him the watch.

As I passed it to him, I noticed his hands. They were the cleanest hands I'd ever seen.

The man's face changed a little when he felt the watch in those clean hands of his, and I felt like I should apologize for the cheap, heavy thing. But before I could say anything, the man said, "No battery for this."

I thought he meant he didn't have the kind of battery it took. I put my hand out to take it back, but now he was studying it.

"Not a bad job," he said, as he looked at the face and then at the back. "Better than the usual ones they bring me here."

"Where can I get a battery?" I asked. I was getting a bit annoyed by all this, and I wanted to get out of the cramped little shop in this questionable part of town.

"I told you," the man said. His tone was sharp. "No battery. It's an automatic."

"What does that mean?"

"It is self-winding."

I didn't really understand what that meant. How could a watch wind itself? I imagined a little hand coming out to wind it up.

The man saw my baffled face and tutted.

"The movement of your arm winds the watch. It's better than a battery. They make good mechanisms in Japan, fair ones in South Korea and Russia, poor ones in China. This is a good fake. I think Japan, which is unusual. Wait here."

He went to the back of his shop and came back with a strange little gadget—a sort of vise with screws and bits sticking out of it. He put it on the counter. He used a tiny screwdriver to take the strap off the watch, and then he put the watch in the vise, clamped it, and turned the handle at the top. This loosened the panel on the back of the watch. The man took it out of the vise, unscrewed the back all the way out with his fingers, and looked at the innards of the watch.

I was interested to see what the insides of a watch were like, and I strained to have a look, but I couldn't see anything.

Then the man reversed the whole process, and handed the watch back to me.

"I suppose you were sent here," he said, his voice level. "Tell whoever sent you that I do not buy stolen goods."

"What?" I said. "No. A man gave this to me. It's only a fake. . . . That's what he did. He sold fakes, knock-offs."

The watch man looked at me. His eyes were very dark, his skin gray. Now he didn't look like he was forty years old. Now he looked ancient.

"Boy, this is a genuine Rolex Submariner," he said. "With a yellow-gold case and strap. It is waterproof down to 1,000 feet. A new one would cost about $33,000. This one dates from the early 1990s and since it has had some damage, it is worth about $16,500. And you tell me a person gave you this watch? Get out please, before I call the police."

I thought about arguing some more, and challenging the man to call the police. Everything I'd said was true. But instead I left the shop. I walked away back down the alley and got the bus home.

And I have the watch still, and I suppose I'll always have it.

I tell people it's a fake. And they believe me because it does look a bit tacky with its gold strap and its midnight-blue face. Unless you know the truth—the truth about watches, the truth about stories, the truth about time.